**En esta casa vive Oso
y ésta es la llave.**

Open the door,
and what do you see?

Abre la puerta,
¿qué es lo que encuentras?

This is the kitchen, all clean and neat,

Ésta es la cocina,
limpia y ordenada.

And this is the dining room, where Bear likes to eat.

Y éste es el comedor,
donde a Oso le gusta comer.

**This is the playroom,
with a big toy chest.**

Éste es el cuarto de juegos, con una caja enorme de juguetes.

And this is the living room, where Bear likes to rest.

Y ésta es la sala,
donde a Oso le gusta descansar.

**This is the hallway,
where Bear climbs the stairs,**

Éste es el pasillo,
por donde Oso sube la escalera.

**And this is the study,
with a big, comfy chair.**

**Y éste es el estudio,
con un grande y cómodo sillón.**

This is the bathroom, with walls painted bright,

Éste es el cuarto de baño,
con paredes muy coloridas.

And this is the bedroom, where Bear says goodnight!

**Y éste es el dormitorio,
donde Oso dice "Buenas noches".**

Downstairs
Planta baja

Playroom

Cuarto de juegos

Dining room

Comedor

Kitchen
Cocina

Living room
Sala

Hallway
Pasillo

Upstairs
Planta alta

Bathroom
Cuarto de baño

Study
Estudio

Bedroom
Dormitorio

Landing
Descanso

Stairs
Escalera

Vocabulary / Vocabulario

tree – el árbol

flower – la flor

oven – el horno

table – la mesa

cat – el gato

sofa – el sillón

mirror – el espejo

book – el libro

bath – el baño

bed – la cama

Barefoot Books
124 Walcot Street
Bath, BA1 5BG, UK

Barefoot Books
2067 Massachusetts Ave
Cambridge, MA 02140, USA

Text copyright © 2001 by Stella Blackstone Illustrations copyright © 2001 by Debbie Harter
Translated by Vicky Cerutti

The moral rights of Stella Blackstone and Debbie Harter have been asserted

First published in Great Britain by Barefoot Books Ltd in 2001 and in the United States of America
by Barefoot Books Inc in 2001. This edition published in 2010

This book has been printed in China by Hung Hing Off-set Printing Ltd on 100% acid-free paper

ISBN 978-1-84686-422-3

1 3 5 7 9 8 6 4 2

British Cataloguing-in-Publication Data:
a catalogue record for this book is available from the British Library

Library of Congress Cataloging-in-Publication Data is available upon request

This is Bear's house, and this is the key.

Bear at Home
Oso en Casa

Stella Blackstone
Debbie Harter